Funny Business

First published in Great Britain by HarperCollins Children's Books in 2010
1 3 5 7 9 10 8 6 4 2
ISBN 978-0-00-736603-3

Based on the television series, Roary the Racing Car and the original script, Funny Business by Chris Parker. Adapted for this publication by Mandy Archer.

A CIP catalogue record for this book is available from the British Library.

The HarperCollins website address is www.harpercollins.co.uk

Visit Roary at www.roarytheracingcar.com

Printed and bound in China.

Funny Business

HarperCollins Children's Books

“Happy days!” bellowed Big Chris, punching the air. “It’s here at last!”

Silver Hatch’s Chief Mechanic carried a large brown parcel into the workshop then proudly plonked it onto his tool cabinet.

“What’s in the box Big Chris?” asked Roary.

Big Chris just shook his head and beckoned for the cars to gather round. “Mama Mia’s coming today, so I want you all looking shiny and neat… Oi!”

The mechanic suddenly stopped talking and clutched the parcel to his chest.

Roary and Maxi slammed on the brakes. They'd been spotted sneaking over for a closer look!

"Leave it alone, will you?" said Big Chris. "You'll find out soon enough what's inside!"

While Big Chris went away to unpack his special delivery, Mr Carburettor was waving Mama Mia through the gates of Silver Hatch racetrack.

"What a day I have planned for you," he announced, before breaking into a long yawn. "First we tour the track, then I take you to a place where they serve spaghetti with the special sauce."

Mr Carburettor helped his mother step out of James, then paused for a sleepy stretch.

Mama Mia shook her head. "My little boy is looking very tired. No rushing around today."

"But Mama!" argued the racetrack owner.

Mama Mia shook her finger. "No working for you," she decided. "Molecom will be my guide!"

Big Chris strolled across the workshop as casually as he could. Every now and then he couldn't help glancing down and sniggering at the big red flower pinned onto his overalls.

"Alright Cici?" he asked. "Do you want a closer look at my flower?"

Cici shrugged. "Er, OK."

The stunt car moved out of her space and turned towards Big Chris. In a trice the mechanic had squeezed the plastic flower, spraying Cici with a shower of cold water.

"Aaah!" squealed Cici. "That was not funny."

But everyone else seemed to think so.

"Ha ha, it's gold dust!" roared Big Chris. "It's my parcel, see? It's a box of jokes and tricks."

Big Chris was on a roll.

"Hey, Marsha!" he called, winking at the cars. "I've got a present for you."

Marsha's face lit up when she saw the nifty telescope in the mechanic's hand.

"Everything's so clear!" she gasped, lifting it to her eye. "Thanks!"

When Marsha put the telescope down, she couldn't see why the cars were shaking with laughter.

Maxi pointed at the big black ring circling her eye. "Fancy falling for a trick like that!" he guffawed.

"You can be so childish," frowned Marsha.

While Big Chris tried not to split his sides, Roary rummaged through the box of jokes. No one noticed him pull out a whoopee cushion and slide it on to Big Chris's chair.

"I think you lot had better go out to play," sighed Marsha.

The cars were happily revving their engines, when Roary suddenly pointed to Maxi's parking bay.

"Wait Maxi!" he cried. "You've got an oil leak!"

The Formula 1 star wailed, but the joke was on him.

"Ha ha!" laughed Roary. "It's only a trick oil puddle from Big Chris's joke box!"

"Nice one Roary!" hooted Big Chris. "I'm going to put these away now. They're just too much fun!"

Maxi frowned at his rival. "I'll get you back for this Roary."

While the cars zoomed about in the sunshine, Mr Carburettor was trying to relax.

"Every time I try and slow down I think of more things to do!" he moaned to Big Chris.

"Why don't you try sitting in my deckchair?" suggested the Chief Mechanic.

The boss nodded. "Maybe I will have fifty winks."

Tin Top passed Cici practising her stunt skids and decided that he owed her an apology.

"I didn't mean to laugh at you earlier," he confessed. "But I sure was tickled!"

Cici smiled craftily. "Oh! I forgot to give you a job from Big Chris. Can you go to Farmer Green's and fetch a tin of elbow grease?"

Tin Top beeped his horn. "Sure thing!"

As soon as they got on the track, Maxi and Roary sped round Quickturn Corner.

Roary called over his shoulder as he overtook. "Sorry about the joke Maxi!"

Maxi's face suddenly dropped. "Look out! Drifter's going to crash into you!"

"Oh no!" cried Roary.

The little red racing car swerved out of control, spinning round and round before landing with a thud in the gravel trap on the side of the course.

"Only joking Roary," sneered Maxi. "That'll teach you to mess with me!"

While Roary and Maxi played jokes on the racetrack, Molecom led Mama Mia up to the commentary tower.

"My poor boy is always working," the grand lady groaned. "All day and all night!"

Molecom nodded. "That's why Mr Carburettor's racetrack runs so smoothly."

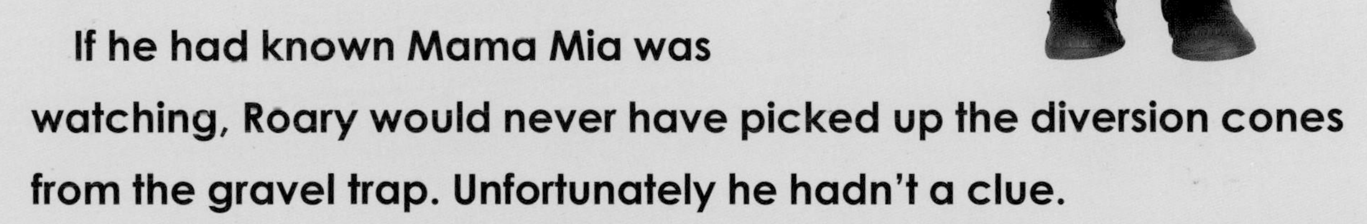

If he had known Mama Mia was watching, Roary would never have picked up the diversion cones from the gravel trap. Unfortunately he hadn't a clue.

"This will teach you to mess with me!" he muttered, setting the cones out across the track.

A few seconds later Maxi sped over Full Throttle Hill.

Molecom could only watch and gasp as the yellow star crashed straight through the cones and into a muddy ditch.

Big Chris was back at the Workshop tinkering with Plugger when his walkie talkie started to beep.

"Maxi's in trouble!" radioed Molecom, trying to keep his voice down so Mama Mia wouldn't overhear.

"What's that?" asked Big Chris. "Right, Plugger and I are on our way!"

Big Chris tiptoed past Mr Carburettor, who had finally fallen asleep.

Farmer Green was very amused when Tin Top pulled into the farm.

"Someone's been having you on!" he chuckled. "Elbow grease doesn't come in tins. It means hard work."

Tin Top rolled his headlights as Cici purred into view. "Bet you think you're pretty funny, don't you?"

Cici giggled as Tin Top chased her round the farmyard. It was all great fun until the cars banged into an enormous stack of hay bales. Straw went everywhere!

Big Chris was not impressed to find Maxi caked in oozy mud. Plugger winched the racing car out of the ditch and back onto the track. Just as the job was finished, Cici and Tin Top drove up.

"What's this?" demanded Big Chris. "First Maxi and now you two covered in straw?"

All the cars started arguing at once.

"STOP!" bellowed Big Chris, starting to understand. "So you put others in danger because of me? I wish I'd never ordered that box of tricks now."

Roary's bonnet drooped. "Sorry, Big Chris."

"Hmm..." grumbled the mechanic, shaking his head. "Maxi, you get washed! The rest of you lot had better clear this straw up before Mama Mia comes."

By the time everyone got cleaned up, Mr Carburettor was awake and showing his mama round the Workshop.

"Molecom has been delightful," announced Mama Mia, sitting down on Big Chris's chair.

Roary gulped. "Er, there's something..."

"Not now," whispered Big Chris, just as Mama Mia's bottom squashed the whoopee cushion and it made a squelchy sound!

The old lady exploded with laughter.

"That's my boy!" she giggled. "You listened to what I said about not working too hard and having some fun eh?!"

Now that everybody was sharing the joke, Marsha wanted to make it clear that she had no hard feelings.

"Here you go Big Chris," she smiled. "I've brought you a flask of tea."

Big Chris beamed and untwisted the lid.

Boiinng! A fuzzy joke snake bounced up to the ceiling.

"Hee hee!" he roared, holding his sides. "Now she's done it to me!"

Name
Mr Carburettor
Home
His mansion, near Silver Hatch Racetrack
Fastest Lap Time
1m 12s
(but only when riding in his chopper, Hellie!)
Top Speed
2.5mph/4kph
Favourite Colour
Purple
Most Likely to Say
Mamma Mia!
Least Likely to Say
Turn off that opera, I wanna hear rock n' roll instead!

Mr
Carburettor

Race to the finish line with these other great Roary books

Out on DVD

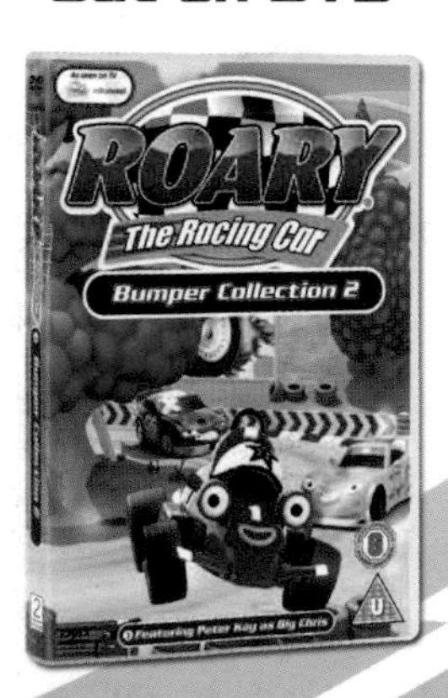

Rescue and recovery out now!

Visit Roary at www.roarytheracingcar.com